Houndsley
and
Catina
and the Birthday Surprise

Houndsley and Catina

and the Birthday Surprise

James Howe

illustrated by Marie-Louise Gay

CANDLEWICK PRESS
CAMBRIDGE, MASSACHUSETTS

for Esme Elizabeth and Phoebe Genevieve
J. H.

Text copyright © 2006 by James Howe
Illustrations copyright © 2006 by Marie-Louise Gay

First paperback edition 2007

The Library of Congress has cataloged the hardcover edition as follows:
Howe, James.
Houndsley and Catina and the birthday surprise / James Howe ;
illustrated by Marie-Louise Gay — 1st ed.
p.   cm.
Summary: Friends Houndsley and Catina are sad because they do not know when their
birthdays are, but they solve the problem in a thoughtful and creative way.
ISBN 978-0-7636-2405-7 (hardcover)
[1. Dogs—Fiction. 2. Cats—Fiction. 3. Birthdays—Fiction. 4. Parties—Fiction.
5. Friendship—Fiction.]   I. Gay, Marie-Louse, ill. II. Title.
PZ7.H83727How 2006
[E]—dc22   2006042580

ISBN 978-0-7636-3640-1 (paperback)

2 4 6 8 10 9 7 5 3 1

Printed in Singapore

This book was typeset in Galliard and Tree-Boxelder.
The illustrations were done in watercolor, pencil, and collage.

Candlewick Press
2067 Massachusetts Avenue
Cambridge, Massachusetts 02140

visit us at www.candlewick.com

Contents

Chapter One
Sad

Houndsley was sad.

"Are you sad because it is raining?"
Catina asked.

Houndsley shook his head.

"I like the rain," he told her.

Catina thought. "Are you sad because there are holes in your sweater?" she asked. Houndsley shook his head again.

"This sweater is very old," he said.
"And moths have to eat, too. I do not feel
sad because there are holes in my sweater."

"Well then, are you sad because you wish you were doing something else?"

Houndsley looked surprised.

"I am never sad because I wish I were doing something else," he told Catina. "If I wanted to be doing something else, I would go and do it."

"Then why are you sad?" asked Catina.

"I am sad because I do not know when my birthday is," Houndsley told his friend.

"Oh," said Catina.

She wanted to say something to cheer Houndsley up.

But all she could think to say was,

"I do not know when my birthday is either."

The two friends walked quietly in the rain until they came to Houndsley's house.

"Do you want to come in?" Houndsley asked.

Catina shook her head. "I should go home," she said.

As he watched her walk away, Houndsley thought, *Oh, dear. Now Catina is sad, too.*

Chapter Two
The Cake

For the next two days, Houndsley did not
see much of Catina. She did not jog by
his house each morning, calling out hello.
She did not invite him to join her each
evening for yoga and ginger tea. He missed
her and worried that something was wrong.

When he bumped into her in town
and asked how she was feeling, Catina said,
"Oh, I'm fine," and hurried away.

Catina does not seem fine, Houndsley
thought. I think she is still sad.

Suddenly, he had an idea.

"I will bake a cake for Catina," he told himself. "A cake will make her feel better."

Houndsley made a list of everything he would need. He even thought to include rainbow sprinkles, which he did not like but he knew Catina loved. Off he went to the market. He could not wait to start baking!

Houndsley was very good at baking, but he always made a mess. It was not long before he was covered in flour and sugar and chocolate.

When his next-door neighbor Bert dropped in, Houndsley explained what he was doing.

"Is it Catina's birthday?" Bert asked.

"No," said Houndsley. "At least, I do not think so. I do not know when Catina's birthday is."

This gave Houndsley another idea. "Bert, will you help me?"

"Of course," said Bert. "By the way, that cake smells yummy. I don't suppose you put any worms in it, did you?"

"I am sorry," Houndsley said. "If I were baking this cake for you, I would have put in worms. But this cake is for Catina, and Catina does not like worms."

Bert shook out his feathers. "We all have our own tastes," he said. "Now, how can I help you?"

"While I finish the cake, will you ask our friends to come to my house tonight at seven o'clock?"

"Are you having a party?" Bert asked.

"Yes," said Houndsley. "A surprise birthday party for Catina. Even though today may not be her birthday."

Bert thought for a moment. "I guess I should not ask Catina to come to your house."

"No," Houndsley said. "I will call Catina later. I will tell her I am still feeling sad and I need her to come over and cheer me up."

"You are very clever," said Bert.

"Thank you," said Houndsley, feeling pleased with himself.

"Well, I'm off," said Bert.

Chapter Three
The Surprise

It took Houndsley the rest of the afternoon
to finish the cake.

"Catina will be so happy," Houndsley
said. "I have never made anything so
beautiful, and I have made it just for her."

He looked around at his messy kitchen
and at the clock on the shelf.

"I will just have time to get everything
cleaned up before the guests arrive,"
he said. "But first I should call Catina."

Just then, the phone rang.

"Hello, Houndsley. This is Catina. I am sorry to bother you, but there is a crack in my bathtub. Could you help me fix it?"

Oh, dear, Houndsley thought. *I cannot say no to a friend who is asking for help.*

"I'll be right there," said Houndsley.

"Thank you," said Catina.

Houndsley thought, *If I can fix the crack in the bathtub really quickly, I will still be able to get Catina to my house by seven o'clock. I will just have to think of an excuse to get her here.*

Houndsley hurried to clean up the mess he had made.

A few minutes before six-thirty, he rang the doorbell of Catina's house.

"I will have to fix that crack quickly," Houndsley told Catina when she opened the door.

But before he could say another word,

he heard "SURPRISE!"

There were all his friends, crowded into Catina's little living room.

Houndsley was confused.

"What about the crack in the bathtub?" he asked.

"There is no crack in the bathtub," said Catina. "I just made that up to get you here."

Then she handed Houndsley a present.

"What is it?" he asked.

"Open it and find out," said Catina.

Houndsley opened the box and pulled out a sweater. A sweater as soft as Houndsley's rose-petal voice. A sweater with no holes made by hungry moths.

"I knitted it for you myself," Catina told Houndsley. "I have not had time to do anything else for the past two days. Happy birthday! Even though today may not be your birthday."

"I have never seen such a beautiful sweater," Houndsley said, slipping it on. It fit perfectly.

Suddenly, Bert rushed in from the kitchen.

"Catina! Houndsley! Something is burning!" he squawked.

Houndsley and Catina ran into the
kitchen. They looked in the oven, but
nothing was burning. They sniffed the air.
Nothing was burning!

"What's the matter with Bert?" Catina
asked.

"And where did everyone go?"
Houndsley said when they went back into
an empty living room.

There was a note on the table:

Houndsley,
you left something
at your house.
Go home and get it.
And bring Catina
with you.
Your friend,
Bert

"Bert is acting very strangely," said
Catina. "I think he has been eating too
many worms."

But Houndsley guessed what Bert was
up to. If he was right, he knew where
everyone had gone.

SURPRISE

all their friends shouted when
Houndsley opened the door
to his house.

"I have never seen such a beautiful cake!" Catina exclaimed.

"I baked it for you myself," Houndsley said proudly.

"I have never been invited to two surprise birthday parties on the same day!" said their friend Moxie.

"We did not know we had the same birthday before this," said Houndsley.

"But we do now," Catina said.

Houndsley showed everyone his new sweater.

Catina blew out the candles on her cake.

And the two friends decided right then and there that every year after that, they would celebrate their birthdays together on the very same day.